NORMAN BRIDWELL
Clifford's
FAMILY

To Shane Stalling

Clifford's FAMILY

Story and pictures by Norman Bridwell

SCHOLASTIC INC.

New York

ISBN 0-590-61734-6

12 11 10 9 8 7 6 5 4 3 2 1   9   5 6 7 8 9/9 0/0
Printed in the U.S.A.   24

I'm Emily Elizabeth, and this is my dog.

His name is Clifford.

We live in a small town now, but we were both born in the city.

One day we went back
to visit our old home
in the city.

CITY
10 MI

Clifford hadn't seen his mother since he was a tiny puppy. She hardly knew him.

She still treated him like a puppy.
She checked his teeth.

And she looked at his ears to see if he had been washing them.

The man told us where Clifford's brother and sisters lived. We went to find them.

Clifford's sister, Claudia, lived nearby.
She was taking her owner for a walk.

We went to the park with them. A taxi was blocking the crosswalk. Clifford took care of that.

Next we found his brother, Nero. Nero was
a rescue dog at a fire station.

While we were there, the alarm rang.
We followed the fire truck. Nero rushed
into the building.

Clifford helped him.

Nero was very brave.

Then we set off to the country. Clifford's
other sister, Bonnie, was a farm dog.

One of Bonnie's jobs was to herd the sheep
into their pen.

Clifford wanted to do some farm work too.

He started to drive the cows toward the barn.

One of the cows was a bull, and bulls
don't like the color red.

Clifford wasn't scared—he was smart.

He didn't want to hurt the bull,

so he jumped out of the way.

When Clifford jumps, he really jumps!

We had one more place to visit. It was Clifford's father's home in a town nearby.

The house was small, and there were a lot
of kids playing in the yard.

Clifford's father didn't have a collar,
or a dog dish, or a dog house. But he
seemed very happy.

Clifford wished his family
could come and live with us.
But they all had people
who needed them...

...just as I need Clifford,
the best dog of all.

I guess it was the kids. He sure loved kids.

He was a lot like Clifford, just a little smaller.

Clifford wished his family
could come and live with us.
But they all had people
who needed them...

...just as I need Clifford,
the best dog of all.